GOD WENT TO BEAUTY SCHOOL

GOD WENT TO
BEAUTY SCHOOL

by

CYNTHIA RYLANT

HARPERTEMPEST
AN IMPRINT OF HARPERCOLLINSPUBLISHERS

HarperTempest is an imprint of
HarperCollins Publishers.

God Went to Beauty School
Copyright © 2003 by Cynthia Rylant
www.harperchildrens.com

Library of Congress Cataloging-in-Publication Data
Rylant, Cynthia.
  God went to beauty school / by Cynthia Rylant
    p.   cm.
  Summary: A novel in poems that reveal God's dis-
covery of the wonders and pains in the world He has
created.
    ISBN-10: 0-06-009435-4
    ISBN-13: 978-0-06-009435-5
    1. God—Fiction. I. Title.
PZ7.R982 Gl 2003   2002069068
[Fic]—dc21   CIP
                                          AC

Typography by Alison Donalty
❖
First HarperTempest paperback edition, 2006

GOD WENT TO BEAUTY SCHOOL

He went there to learn how
to give a good perm
and ended up just crazy
about nails
so He opened up His own shop.
"Nails by Jim" He called it.
He was afraid to call it
Nails by God.
He was sure people would
think He was being
disrespectful and using
His own name in vain
and nobody would tip.
He got into nails, of course,
because He'd always loved
hands—
hands were some of the best things
He'd ever done
and this way He could just
hold one in His
and admire those delicate
bones just above the knuckles,
delicate as birds' wings,
and after He'd done that
awhile,

He could paint all the nails
any color He wanted,
then say,
"Beautiful,"
and mean it.

He never meant to.
He liked dogs, He'd
liked them ever since He was a kid,
but He didn't think
He had time for a dog now.
He was always working
and dogs needed so
much attention.
God didn't know if He
could take being needed
by one more thing.
But He saw this dog
out by the tracks
and it was hungry
and cold
and lonely
and God realized
He'd made that dog
somehow,
somehow He was responsible
though He knew logically
that He had only set the
world on its course.
He couldn't be blamed
for everything.

But He saw this dog
and He felt bad
so He took it on home
and named it Ernie
and now God
has somebody
keeping His feet warm at night.

And said "Wow."
He'd never actually
floated in a boat, though
He'd seen people
out on the water and
told Himself He'd have
to try that someday.
Water had always bored Him
until He started seeing
people having fun on it.
So one day He got in a boat,
said Wow,
and headed out across the lake.
And the whole world looked different.
He couldn't get over it.
It didn't look anything like
it looked from the sky
or from the ground
or even from inside a whale,
which He'd tried once or twice.
He sat in the boat
and was surprised how
much sense it all made.
All the little houses
and all the green trees

and all the tidy cities
and all the sky and all the land,
it all made sense.
He was surprised.
Because, really,
He'd just been winging it.

He ordered it from Pottery Barn
and He had a little trouble
because His credit card
billing address didn't match
the delivery address.
They weren't totally convinced
He was God.
Because for one thing
He got His credit card
bills in Hell
(just His quirky
sense of humor)
and He wanted the
couch shipped to Heaven
(the old one was too hard),
but they didn't buy it
until He told them
how He made the first
rhinoceros.
He had it all down,
the DNA, the chromosomes,
and especially the
Holy Spirit.
Nobody is as convincing
about the Holy Spirit

as God.
They asked Him did
He want corduroy or leather.
He said, "What do
you think?"

And He didn't have a ceiling
so He tried to make it stick
to Jupiter
but that just
vaporized the noodle
so God decided to
HAVE FAITH it was cooked
al dente.
He filled up a big bowl
and got Himself a
piece of sourdough
and a copy of
The New Yorker
and God
had supper.
And He would actually
have liked somebody
to talk to
(He didn't like eating alone),
but most people
think God
lives on air
(apparently they've not noticed
all the *food* He's created),
so nobody ever

invites him over
unless it's Communion
and that's always
such a letdown.
God's gotten used
to one plate at the table.
He lights a candle
anyway.

And the doctor said,
"You don't need me,
you're God."
And God said,
"Well, you're pretty good
at playing me,
I figured you'd
know what the
problem was."
So the doctor
examined Him.
He couldn't find
anything wrong
except a little
skip in God's heart.
"Probably nothing,"
he told God.
"But eat more fish."
God sighed.
He was hoping
for more than that.
Maybe an antibiotic.
Or a shot.
He knew about that
skip in His heart.

He knew it was nothing
fish would cure.
The skip had started way back,
when He first heard
that some people
didn't believe in Him.
It scared Him. Still does.

But they didn't
know it was Him
because He had on
His disguise.
It was His guy-disguise.
He was actually
pretty proud of it.
It had a tattoo
around the belly button
(which hurt!).
Anyway, He got arrested
because He got
into a fight in a bar
when somebody said
something about
Jesus Christ except
not in a good way
at all.
Might as well have
insulted God's mother
(now that's a whole
other story), because
God—who was only there
because He liked
the jukebox—

lost it.
And his anger erupted like
the wrath of . . .
Oh, *right*. Never mind.
Just be careful
dropping names
in Kenny's Tavern.
Might be next to a relative.

And He was groggy
so He got a nice cup of coffee
and went to sit
under an apple tree.
He sat there
drinking His coffee,
listening to the birds,
when all of a sudden
it hit Him.
He was happy.
God was *happy!*
And He wished there
was just someone to see it.
He'd gotten such a bad rap
all these years
for being pissed off
all the time.
And He really wasn't.
Maybe a little *cranky.*
But here He was,
happy.
Mellow yellow.
The birds were singing
and He was at peace.
Buddha told Him it

could be this way,
but He'd never really
believed it until now.
Life really was easier,
sitting under a tree.

With His clothes on.
His robe, to be specific.
Why did He do this?
He was shy,
that's why.
A little self-conscious
about His body.
God wasn't always
this way.
He used to be free as a bird,
running stark naked
everywhere.
He never thought
about bodies at all.
Then these things
started coming back to Him:
The whole misunderstanding
with Adam and Eve.
Then circumcision.
Then talk talk talk
of everybody being made
in His image.
Until He got afraid
to look in a mirror.
Everybody had such

high expectations
and now He was
a little insecure.
Could be He was flabby.
Love handles on God
would have to be *huge*.
So He kept His robe on.

He loved it.
He wasn't very good at it.
He fell twenty times.
But God always
bounces back.
"Cool!" said God
as He whooshed
past the old ladies.
He felt
invincible.
(He knew He *was*
invincible
but He didn't
always feel that way.
Not every day.)
God made some other
friends on
Rollerblades.
God thought
they were
way cool.
He was proud
of them.
Proud that they
flew their spirits

down the alleys
and the boardwalks
and the streets
like angels.
They were, you know.
And they
hadn't forgotten.

And He was such a baby.
He *never* caught colds.
He loved to brag about it.
And now here He was:
snot nosed.
It's hard to be
authoritative
with a cold.
It's hard to
thunder
"THOU SHALT NOT!"
when it comes out
"THOU SHALT DOT!"
Nobody takes Him
seriously.
And besides,
He wanted some comic books
and juice
and somebody to be
nice to Him.
He called up His
old friend
Mother Theresa.
He asked her to
come over and see Him.

He asked could she
bring some comic books.
And of course she did.
Mother Theresa loves
all who suffer.
Even God.
Maybe Him a little more.

And it made Him cry and cry.
He couldn't get over it.
He'd seen all the worst
stuff in real life.
But this just
knocked Him out.
He was mystified.
He decided to go
find the guy
who wrote the film.
He did,
and He looked into his heart.
Normal heart.
He decided to go
find the guy
who directed the film.
He did,
and He looked into his heart.
Normal heart.
Then He went to see
the guy who did the music.
Sure enough: normal heart.
Then He went to see
the producer.
He asked him why normal hearts

had made God cry.
And the producer said,
"It's a mystery."
Well. God understood *that*.
He didn't go looking for
anybody else.
Just went home and cried.

No, not *that* one.
Everybody thinks He
wrote *that* one,
but He didn't.
He's a better writer
than that.
Those guys just
went on and on
and did they
bother to edit?
No.
But wouldn't you know,
you mention a name
and you're in.
So they said,
"*I* didn't write it,
God wrote it."
A sure way
to get out of revising.
But God wrote
His *own* book.
He wrote it for
one little boy.
Just one.
He read it to the boy

at bedtime
because the boy couldn't sleep.
So God read him a book.
The boy grew up. He became a writer.
Which one?
Not telling.

And for a week
watched nothing but.
Didn't see the comet.
Didn't see the hurricane.
Missed that baby
being born entirely.
Just watched cable.
Funny thing is,
He liked it.
He knew He wasn't
supposed to.
All those girls
crying about their
boyfriends.
All those track meets.
All that
soap and toothpaste.
He liked it.
Couldn't help it.
Then Gabriel came
over with a deck of cards
and next thing you know,
they've played poker
four weeks straight.
Gabriel's beard nearly

as long as God's
and corn chips all over the place.
And what God decided was that
he liked not *cable*,
not *poker*,
but a break.
Every now and then,
even God needs a break.

It was the *weirdest* thing.
God got all religious
on Himself.
He was looking for
something to do
so He went into this
church in Boston.
One of those churches
from the 1800s that
likes to consider
itself *old*.
(This always gives
God a good laugh.)
And He was all by Himself
and it was quiet
like you wouldn't believe,
and up to the sky
went these beautiful rafters,
and all around Him
were these beautiful stained glass windows
and everybody was praying.
All the people in the pictures,
all the statues,
all the angels in the room,
were praying.

God knew better than to look
at any of the crosses.
He was still trying to figure
that all out.
But He knew that He
had actually found a Holy Place.
So He dropped a coin in the
Building Fund box, before He went away.

And not just any mountain.
Mount Everest.
And you know why?
BECAUSE IT WAS THERE.
He was tired of hearing about it—
He decided just to
go do it.
And He did.
It was terrible.
It was awful.
He'd never been so cold.
He'd never been so tired.
He *hated* snow.
And it was like that
all the way to
the top.
Then at the top
He turned around
and His heart just broke.
Suddenly the whole world
was plain as day,
and still.
It was so still.
"Should've put everybody
on top of Mount Everest,"

God thought.
Nobody'd want to hit
the guy next to him
on top of Mount Everest.
"Next time," thought God.
Next time.

Though nobody wants
to talk about it.
Nobody wants to *think*
about it.
Not even God.
He knows He's a guy, too.
He knows He's lots of things.
He's an eagle.
He's a tree.
On less than wonderful days
He's even a pig.
God's a lot of things.
But He likes His guyness best.
People who know Him
know this,
so they always refer to Him as "He."
Sometimes they call him "Bob."
He isn't sure why.
But God does guy stuff.
He wears guy cologne.
He listens to guy music.
He eats guy food.
God can't help it.
He wants to be a guy.
Which is why,

whenever He gets the urge
to watch reruns of *Sisters*,
He's embarrassed.
He lights a big cigar
and spits.

Lucy, or Lucifer,
if you want to be formal.
Everybody called him
Lucy growing up,
which accounts a lot
for how he turned out.
God's not as mad at him
as some people think.
You don't become God
by holding grudges.
And besides,
Lucy taught Him
how to swing a bat,
though nobody wants
to hear about that.
Living in the same neighborhood,
hanging at the same places,
you get to feeling close,
you know?
Lucy's one of the few people
left who remember
what it was like
In The Beginning.
Sure, God and he went
their separate ways,

but truth be known,
they're always asking,
"How's he doing?" and "How's He doing?"
That's the way it is
with family.
God's still looking
for Lucy to move back.

Just to see what it
would be like.
Made his back hurt.
God's always had a
bad back anyway—
the weight of the world
and all that.
He thought *His* job was tough,
'til He sat at a desk all day.
It was torture.
He could feel the Light
inside Him grow
dimmer and dimmer
and He thought that
if He had to pick
up that phone
one more time,
He'd just start the
whole Armageddon thing
people keep talking about.
(Not His idea, not His plan,
but in a pinch, He's
sure He can come up
with something.)
The only thing that got

Him through to the
end of the day was
Snickers bars.
He ate thirty-seven.
Plus thinking about the Eagle Nebula
in the constellation Serpens.
That helped.

In the mail.
It was from an
archangel who'd been
through the Denver airport
and had it shipped
out from there.
The candy store thought
they'd sent it to
Grants Pass, Oregon.
Well, more goes on
in Grants Pass
than you might think.
Like *God UPS.*
But anyway—
He got the fudge
and He liked it.
So He thought He'd
make some of His own.
But everything God
does tends to turn out big.
Really big.
God's fudge wouldn't harden
so He kept stirring it
and stirring it,
and when He dropped it

in some water
to see if it formed
a ball,
it made
Neptune.
Or that's what it's called now.
God called it fudge.

To this country music
singer He liked.
God *rarely* writes fan letters,
so He figured the singer
would make a
big deal out of this.
He figured He'd get
an autographed photo
or something.
But she never wrote back.
Nothing.
So He wrote her again.
And He signed it
"God. *Really.*"
Nothing.
Finally He wrote
one last time.
He told her how much
He liked her singing
and how He had her
concert video, which
He played over and over,
and how, if she wanted,
He could answer her prayers.
Well—one at least.

And finally, *finally*
she wrote back.
And she said,
"Dear God, I pray
you will get a life."
Well, thought God.
Just what did she mean by that?

To see the elephants.
God adores elephants.
He thinks they are
the best thing
He ever made.
They do everything
He hoped for:
They love their children,
they don't kill,
they mourn their dead.
This last thing is
especially important
to God.
Elephants visit the graves
of those they loved.
They spend hours there.
They fondle the dry bones.
They mourn.
God understands mourning
better than any other emotion,
better even than love.
Because He has lost
everything He has
ever made.
You make life,

you make death.
The things God makes
always turn into
something else and
He does find this good.
But He can't help missing all the originals.

Sort of.
It's a long story.
But if you have time . . .
Okay—
God has been God
for so long
even *He* doesn't have
a clue where He
came from.
For a while He
wasn't even sure
He *was* God, until
everything He said
or thought or
wanted to happen
happened.
That was a big tip-off.
So He didn't remember
where He came from
or why.
He just knew
what He could do.
Oh, He wanted to be
very careful with this.

This could be Good.
This could be the
biggest thing in the
universe.
He just had to be
a really tip-top God.
Somebody who made
no mistakes.
Who didn't show up
late for work.
Who competed
only against Himself.
He could do this.
He was GOD.
So He thought about
everything
for a really really
really really really
long time.
Then He opened His mouth
and said,
"Let There Be Light."
And it was so.
Good, said God.
And after that
no one could stop Him.

He said "Let There Be"
a billion trillion zillion
times and when He
was finished,
there were so many
new things, even *He*
didn't know
what some of them were.
(Like grapefruit spoons.)
But it was all Good.
Really good, said God.
Then who knows what
went wrong, but
one morning God woke up
and His right-hand angel
at the time (Sheila)
said, "You know those
two brothers? One
just killed the other."
God could not
believe this.
He *could not*
believe this.
(It should be mentioned
that this was
way before Lucy

relocated to more
southern regions.)
God, in fact,
did not even know
exactly what
"killed" meant,
until Sheila explained it
very carefully to Him.
Even then, He had
to see for Himself.
And there He saw
that boy—Abel
was his name—
covered with blood
and not a hint of
life in him.
Not a whiff.
God wanted to start
all over again,
make everything
all over again,
from scratch.
Make it so nothing
in this world
could be "killed."
But Sheila said,

"You can't start over.
You'd have to
kill everything
to start over."
God hadn't considered this.
God lived purely in the moment
so He wasn't the greatest
long-range planner.
But He stopped and
thought about what
Sheila said, and
though there were
some things He could
probably kill
and feel pretty
okay about it
(He wasn't all that attached to
the chicken pox virus,
for example),
there were other things
He could not ever
let go.
Sea turtles, for one.
Spiders, for another.
Too beautiful, too beautiful,
He said.

What to do?
God was like anybody else.
Everything was the
first time for Him, too.
He didn't mean to make
what happened between
Abel and his brother
happen.
He thought they'd be
good buddies.
Like ducks.
Hadn't they learned
anything from ducks?
Apparently not.
God was stricken.
He *did not know*
what to do.
If He left things as
they were,
there was bound to be
more killing.
Could He bear this?
God's blood was love.
His bones were love.
His eyes, his heart,
his kidneys were love.

He didn't know
what He'd done wrong
that caused a thing—the other brother—
to be born
without love.
A thing
that came from *Him*.
He asked Sheila
what she thought
He should do,
now that killing
was a part of things.
And Sheila said, "Die."
Just like that.
Sheila had always been
a very smart girl.
So the story goes
that God took on
the blood, the bones,
the eyes, the heart, the
kidneys of a man.
And He made real friends.
And He loved a real family.
And He prayed real prayers.
He didn't go unnoticed.
Ever after, religions were made

that insisted that God
had been this guy or that guy
or the other.
But one thing happened
for sure.
God died.
No one knows precisely how.
But sure enough,
He did it.
Because it was the
only way He could
find out what it is
to love
a drink of water,
sleep,
a warm coat,
a mother,
a father,
morning,
evening,
a really good joke.
And pain.
God saw so much pain
and He was sorry for it.
He didn't know it would
happen quite that way,

but He finally saw
how pain caused
one of two things:
A reverence for life.
Or killing.
Both grew from the same seed.
The one He had planted.
So God went back
to being God,
finally comfortable
with being called
All-Knowing
because now
He actually was.
And after that,
He made sure
He ate popcorn and
watched a movie
every Friday night.
Petted the cats.
Fed the birds.
And played the jukebox
at Kenny's Tavern.
God needed
to remember
what a cool thing

it was to be a guy.
Or a girl.
An eagle.
A pig.
To be life.
God went to beauty school.
He went there to learn how
to give a good perm.
But what He was really there for
was the *hands*.